For Patricia, Oréo, and the Pépette
— J.-P. A.-V.

To Basile
— O. T.

First published in the United States in 2009 by Chronicle Books LLC.

Text © 2006 by Jean-Philippe Arrou-Vignod.
Illustrations © 2006 by Olivier Tallec.
Translation © 2009 by Chronicle Books LLC.
Originally published in France in 2006 by Gallimard Jeunesse under the title
Rita et Machin à la Plage.

North American type design by Natalie Davis.
Typeset in The Serif Semi Light.
Manufactured in China.

Library of Congress Cataloging-in-Publication Data
Arrou-Vignod, Jean-Philippe, 1958–
[Rita et Machin à la plage. English]
Rita and Whatsit at the beach / by Jean-Philippe Arrou-Vignod ; illustrated
by Olivier Tallec.
p. cm.
Summary: Rita and her sometime talking dog, Whatsit, spend an adventur-
ous day at the beach.
ISBN 978-0-8118-6551-7
[1. Beaches—Fiction. 2. Dogs—Fiction.] I. Tallec, Olivier, ill. II. Title.
PZ7.A74339Rm 2009
[E]—dc22
2008039586

10 9 8 7 6 5 4 3 2 1

Chronicle Books LLC
680 Second Street, San Francisco, California 94107

www.chroniclekids.com

By JEAN-PHILIPPE ARROU-VIGNOD ✳ Illustrated by OLIVIER TALLEC

chronicle books · san francisco

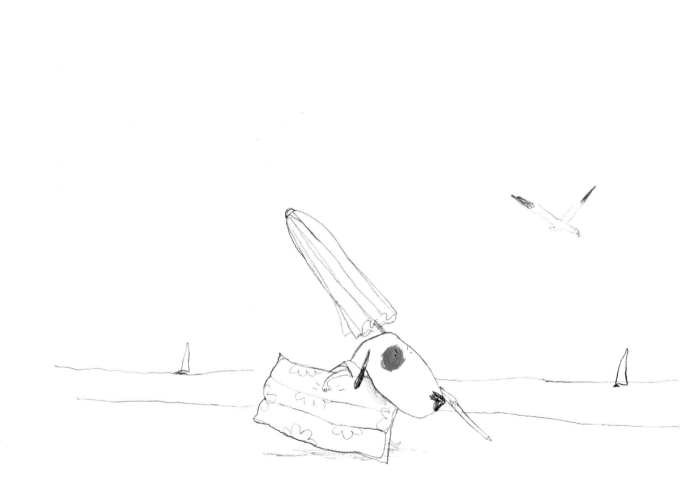

Rita *loves* the beach.
Whatsit the dog doesn't like it *quite* so much.

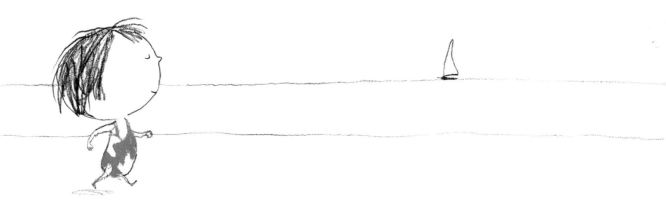

Rita has a new swimsuit. Whatsit has one, too—one that Rita made for him.

"OK, so it sags a little. You don't want to swim *naked*, do you?"

Rita has lots of things she wants to do today:

1. fly a kite

2. go for a pedal boat ride

3. build a beautiful sand castle and pretend she's Princess Bikini

Whatsit is not interested.

The things Whatsit likes about the beach are:

1. chasing the crabs

2. eating sugary things until he's all sticky

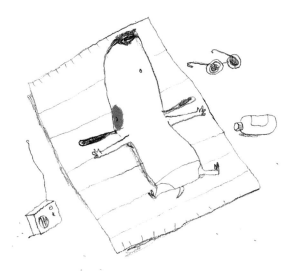

3. making like a pancake
   for the rest of the day

"Whatsit! Where are you?

I'm warning you, if you don't get back here,
I'll change your name to Chicken Giblets!"

But Whatsit has disappeared.
Rita is a little worried.

"Has anyone seen a puppy
without a name?"

Suddenly, between one wave and the next,
Rita sees something.

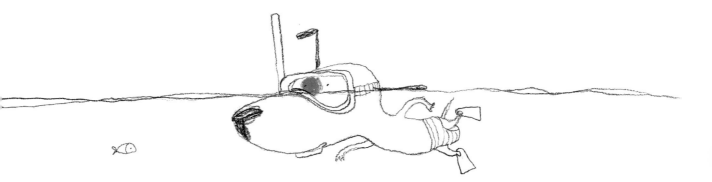

Watch out, Rita! A submarine! It's going to attack
Princess Bikini's castle!

Rita recognizes that submarine. Beneath its decks hides
Captain Whatsit, chief henchman for Queen Catastrophe,
the most dangerous dog in the galaxy!

"En garde, Captain Whatsit!

I'll defend my castle to the death!

...But no throwing sand, OK?"

Princess Bikini runs away, but Captain Whatsit is in hot pursuit.

"You'll never take me alive, Captain Whatsit!

…But no splashing, OK?"

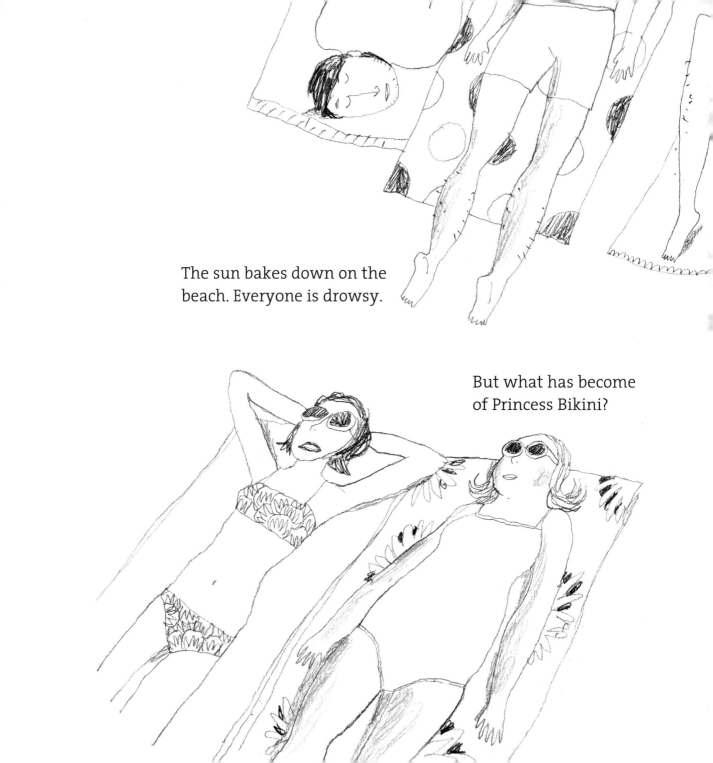

The sun bakes down on the beach. Everyone is drowsy.

But what has become of Princess Bikini?

She's taken refuge in a deep, dark cave! It's just too hot out to fight an enemy as powerful and devious as Captain Whatsit.

"Spare my life," begs Princess Bikini, "and I'll give you whatever you want!"

"OK," says Captain Whatsit. "I want a three-scoop ice cream cone . . .
and a donut with lots of sugar . . ."

"Ice cream *and* a donut?"

"...And a large soda
with two ice cubes,
a straw, and a
slice of lemon."

"Augh!"

All things considered, Whatsit really loves the beach.
Rita doesn't like it *quite* so much.

But Princess Bikini isn't defeated yet. Tomorrow, Captain Whatsit won't know what hit him!